The Pirate of Creole Bay

Mike Holliday

FishingKids
White Bear Lake, Minnesota

The **Pirate** of Creole Bay

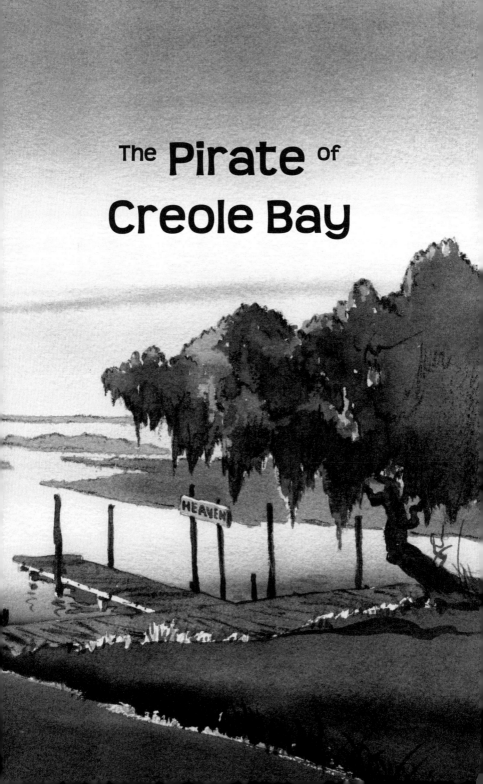

FishingKids
PO Box 10590,
White Bear Lake, MN 55110
www.fishingkids.com

Library of Congress Control Number: 2012933136

Credits
Cover and Interior Illustrations
Olga and Aleksey Ivanov

Spinner's Notebook Sketches and Map
Marilyn Emma Anderson

Creative Direction
Megan Derbes McCarthy

Layout and Design
Flat Sole Studio

Printed in the United States of America in Stevens Point, Wisconsin

Table of Contents

Crawdaddy's

Bayou Perot

Spinner Family Campsite

Shrimp's House

Bayou Boudreaux's House

Vulture Island

Heaven

Spanish Moss

Shrimp's Dad's
Shrimp boat

Creole Bay,
Louisiana

Bobber and I were walking up from the dock when we spotted the Zephyr parked at The Chief's house. "Zephyr" was the name Uncle Pete gave his tricked-out RV.

"Looks like your grandfather is planning another fishing trip with your Uncle Pete," said Bobber as he pointed to the recreational vehicle. "Your Uncle Pete doesn't bring the Zephyr over unless they're planning on going somewhere."

"You're right, Bobber!" I answered. We started running towards The Chief's open garage door.

When we got to the garage, The Chief was at his work bench. He had a spinning reel taken apart and was greasing the gears inside the reel. We tried to act casual as we glanced around looking for Uncle Pete. He was nowhere to be seen.

"Hey, Chief!" I said. "What'cha doing?"

"Just working on one of my fishing reels. Got to keep them in good working order if I want to use them to fish," said The Chief. My grandfather takes great care of his fishing gear. He has rods and reels from years ago that still work perfectly.

"We just caught some fish down on the dock," I boasted.

"I caught a two-pound smallmouth with my Shoe Bait!" reported Bobber.

"That's a nice fish for a warm summer morning," said The Chief matter-of-factly, and then he went back to working on the reel.

Bobber nudged me with his elbow.

"Um, yeah, but nothing like the fish we catch when we go on a fishing trip with you and Uncle Pete," I said, hinting at the possibility of a new fishing adventure. "I sure wish we could go on another one someday soon."

The Chief didn't even look up. Instead, he just smiled, nodded his head, and started putting the reel back together.

We stood there for awhile waiting for The Chief to say more, and it was really silent for a long time. I started to feel kind of awkward when all of a sudden the door leading into the house burst open with a *WHOOSH!* and washed away the uncomfortable silence. Out stepped Uncle Pete.

At least, I think it was Uncle Pete. He had on blue jean overalls with the legs tucked into white rubber boots, a camouflage sweatshirt, and the head of an alligator with its mouth open pulled down over his face.

"Who dat be wantin' to go a-fishin'?" he said. "We got us some bandy crawfish he'ah!"

The Chief burst out laughing as he saw the look of shock on our faces.

"Great gaping gator jaws, it's the swamp-faced fisherman!" Bobber shouted excitedly.

"Nah, it's only Uncle Pete," I said, moving closer so I could lift up the nose of the alligator mask and see his face. "Why are you dressed up like a gator trapper and talking like that, Uncle Pete?"

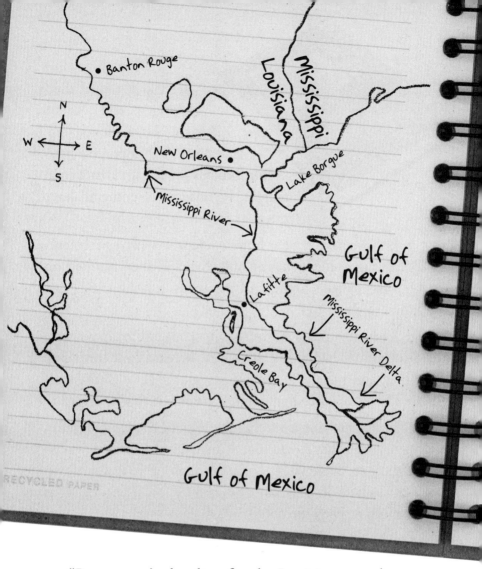

Banton Rouge

Louisiana

Mississippi

N
W ← → E
S

New Orleans

Lake Borgue

Mississippi River

Gulf of
Mexico

Lafitte

Mississippi River Delta

Creole Bay

Gulf of Mexico

RECYCLED PAPER

"Because we're heading for the Louisiana marshes —
Sportsman's Paradise! — where the bass and redfish swim
together with the alligators, and there's more water than
land," he replied. "So I'm practicing my Cajun accent for
our trip."

"Ha ha, HEAD-ing for Louisiana! Get it? And he's
wearing a gator head? Good one, Uncle Pete," laughed
Bobber.

"I thought you'd get a kick out of that, Bobber," said Uncle Pete as he removed the gator head. "I hope you boys like boiled crawfish and blackened redfish, because we're going to have us a regular Cajun fishing trip!"

Bobber and I were both overcome with excitement. Bobber gave me a rushed high five and then jumped on his bike to ride home and get ready for the trip. I ran home to pack, too.

The first thing I stuffed into my suitcase was my FishingKids Notebook. It was a Christmas gift from The Chief, and I use it to write down all the cool fishing stuff that I learn and to make notes about our fishing trips.

In my room, I looked at the map of the United States on my wall just to get a feel for where Louisiana was in relation to White Bear Lake, Minnesota. It is way down south where it is warm and steamy. So I packed light clothing to keep me cool.

I had just finished when Bobber's parents dropped him off. He walked in carrying a suitcase that looked like it was going to burst. It was more round than square, had clothes sticking out the sides, and his favorite fishing hat wrapped around the handle.

"Gee, Bobber, you didn't have to bring everything you own," I said, pointing to the ruler sticking out from among the clothes. "Are you planning on doing some geometry with that?"

"That's my brand new FishingKids Fish Ruler," he said proudly while stuffing it back into the suitcase. "We can use it to measure the gigant-o fish we're gonna catch. I'm gonna catch a fish so big we have to use three rulers to measure it!"

One thing I love about Bobber is that he always sets his goals high.

"Well, I hope you have some clothes in that bag, or else by the end of the trip, we'll be measuring how far we have to stay away from you in order to breathe," I said with a smile.

"I know. I know," said Bobber. "I was so excited, I even packed the sandwich my mom made me for lunch. If I hadn't seen jelly squeeze out the side of my suitcase when I shut it, the sandwich would still be in there."

We both laughed at his near disaster, grabbed our bags, and then headed outside. Next to Uncle Pete's RV we saw two more suitcases.

"Gee, Spinner, did you pack everything you own?" asked Bobber.

"Those aren't my suitcases. My mom grew up in Louisiana, so she and my dad are coming, too," I told Bobber. "This is going to be the best fishing trip ever!"

Chapter 1

Po-Boys

Bobber and I began loading up the Zephyr. Now, Uncle Pete's RV isn't an ordinary RV. It's like a plane on wheels, and mounted on the Zephyr's front is a big wooden propeller that spins when we get going real fast. Also, on the roof are two big plastic bubbles that we can look out as we're zipping down the highway.

"The Zephyr only has two beds and two fold-out couches. Where will everyone sleep?" I asked Uncle Pete as he came over to help us.

He explained that my mom and The Chief would sleep in the RV. The rest of us would pitch tents and camp outside. Next to fishing, camping is one of my all-time-favorite activities. Getting to combine fishing and camping just made this vacation even better.

"We can fish all day and then stay up late by the fire eating marshmallows," said Bobber. "Yum! Fish and marshmallows. Hey, we could create a new snack food:

FISHMALLOWS! We'll be the Legendary Tent Camping Fishmallow Inventing Champs of Louisiana!"

"Ew," declared my mom as she entered the Zephyr. "Fishmallows don't sound so good to me. I'll just have the normal s'mores if that's okay with you guys."

"Mrs. Pinner, everything is better with marshmallows!" said Bobber. "The only way my mom got me to try brussel sprouts was by melting marshmallows on top of them. I come from a long line of mad scientist marshmallow inventors. How about shrimpmallows?" asked Bobber. "Aren't the marshes full of shrimp?"

Shrimp, crabs, fish — my mom said that the marsh is teeming with life. She also said that there are snapping turtles, snakes, alligators, and nutria.

"We could make turtle soup, a Louisiana specialty," said Mom.

"Snapping turtle stew?" said Bobber. "No thanks, Mrs. Pinner. I don't eat anything that bites. And no snakes or alligators or new trees either."

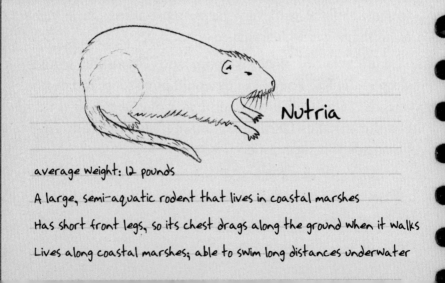

Nutria

average weight: 12 pounds

A large, semi-aquatic rodent that lives in coastal marshes

Has short front legs, so its chest drags along the ground when it walks

Lives along coastal marshes; able to swim long distances underwater

"Not *new trees*, Bobber. Nutria," explained Mom. "They're like a cross between a rat and an otter."

"Okay, I'm sleeping on the Zephyr's roof," announced Bobber. "I don't want snapping turtles or otter rats nibbling on my toes while I'm sleeping."

My mom laughed at Bobber being Bobber, and then told us what to expect on our trip down to Louisiana. She talked about the Acadian people — known as Cajuns — who came to Louisiana from France hundreds of years ago. The Cajun culture is rich and proud, my mom said, and she was excited to introduce us to it. She also explained that the language we would hear is a unique type of French found only in South Louisiana.

"The people of Louisiana live off the land," said Mom as she rubbed her stomach. "Just wait until you try the po-boys, seafood gumbo, jambalaya, and beignets. Ooo-ee! I can almost smell the chicory coffee brewing."

Just then, The Chief walked in carrying a tent and lantern. He shook the tent and little pieces of cloth flew into the air. It looked pitiful.

Cajun Food

* beignet (pronounced "bin-YAY") - fried dough with powdered sugar
* gumbo - a stew with okra and seafood
* jambalaya - a spicy and hearty rice dish
* po-boy - a sandwich (usually seafood, like fried shrimp or fried oysters) on crusty French bread

"I don't know if moths got this tent or if it is just worn out from use," said The Chief. "But we'll have to stop at a store in Louisiana, to get a new one, and maybe a new sleeping bag or two."

"Does that store have snapping turtle or otter rat repellent? If so, I brought some of my allowance, and I'm going to buy a whole gallon of it to soak my clothes in," said Bobber. "No swamp critters are going to sneak into my tent if I can help it."

With a wink, The Chief said, "I'd be more worried about pirates and the ghost of Jean Lafitte. The animals will likely leave you alone."

"G-g-g-g-ghosts?" said Bobber. "Pirates!? That's it. I'm going to get a pop-up tent and put it on the roof of the Zephyr where the ghost pirates can't see me and the gators and the nutra-rats can't reach me!"

The Chief laughed, put his arm around Bobber, and assured him that pirates wouldn't come into camp. They're more likely, he said, to be out on the marsh looking for buried treasure.

Chapter 2

Stinky Lafitte

The minutes and the miles rolled by as the Zephyr bounded south down the highway towards Louisiana.

"There's the Arkansas state line," said Uncle Pete, pointing to a sign on the side of the road. "Our mission is one state away in Cajun country."

Uncle Pete called our trips "missions," like the trips he would take when he was a pilot for the military years ago. He was sitting behind the wheel of the Zephyr in his air-cooled captain's chair.

The Chief was sitting on the couch, my dad was at the computer desk, and Bobber and I sat in the big lounge chairs studying our FishingKids Fish Identification Cards. We had sorted out the ones with the marine life we would find in Louisiana. It's always good to be prepared, and we like to impress The Chief with what we know when we are out fishing with him. My mom was up late packing, so she was in the back of the Zephyr taking a nap.

"Hey Chief, will you tell us more about Jean Lafitte and his buried treasure?" asked Bobber. "If we find a treasure chest, we could buy a bunch of new fishing tackle, or a new boat!"

"I want to know more about his ghost," I said.

"Isn't the town we're going called Lafitte?" asked Bobber. "Was he a king of Louisiana or something?"

"No, Bobber, but he is an important part of Louisiana history," explained The Chief, "Although his name is spelled J-E-A-N, the French pronunciation is more like John, and Jean Lafitte was a famous slave trader and greedy pirate. Rumor has it that he once sailed a ship full of Napoleon Bonaparte's treasure from France to Louisiana, and Lafitte buried the treasure all over the bayou."

"Napoleon, the Emperor of France, right?" interrupted Bobber. "He's that short guy who always has one hand tucked inside his shirt."

"Right, Bobber," said The Chief. "Now people say they see the ghost of Jean Lafitte sailing the bayou at night. That he's guarding the hidden bounty to this very day."

"Whoa! Wouldn't it be cool to search for buried treasure?" I said, my heart pumping with excitement.

"Not if the pirate ghost of Jean Lafitte is guarding it!" said Bobber. "Pirates and ghosts are not a good combination. I think I'll just stick to fishing and leave the pirates alone."

"You're not likely to run into any pirates on this trip, boys," said Dad as he pulled out a map of the town of Lafitte. "If you look at the map, most of the area is surrounded by shallow water that flows out of the marshes

Jean Lafitte (1775–1823)

He was a French pirate in Louisiana who smuggled stolen goods. He called himself a "privateer" instead of a "pirate" and would challenge anyone to a duel who called him a pirate to his face. He helped General Andrew Jackson defeat the British in the Battle of New Orleans (1815)

and lakes to the north and into the Gulf of Mexico. These marshes are too shallow for a pirate ship."

"But, they're a perfect place for a small boat like *The Water Zephyr*," Uncle Pete called out from the captain's chair.

Uncle Pete's boat, named *The Water Zephyr*, is a 22-foot Lowe aluminum V-hull with a 90-horsepower

outboard motor. It was hooked to the back of the RV, and we knew it was going to get plenty of use on this trip. The town of Lafitte looked like a long piece of land surrounded by creeks and small lakes called bayous, and one large bay that they all emptied into.

Dad explained that all the little creeks and canals in the marsh drain through the bayous and into Creole Bay. Shrimp and Coccahoe minnows, which are small baitfish, grow up in the shallows of the marsh, and then move into the bay as they get bigger.

He told us how the redfish and flounder move up into the marsh to eat the small shrimp and minnows. And he

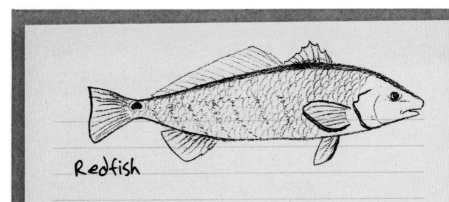

Redfish

Average length: 18 - 24 inches   Average weight: 6 - 8 pounds
Bait: shrimp, crab, mullet, soft plastic jerkbaits, topwater plugs
Dark red backs, white bellies, and a black spot on their tails
Also called red drum, spottail bass, reds, puppy drum

talked about the big trout in the canals and open water like Creole Bay, where Jean Lafitte would stop to resupply his boats with food and water.

"I bet that's where the ghost of Jean Lafitte lives," I said. "Do you think we'll see him sailing his pirate ship?"

"Not likely," said Dad. "He's been dead for a long time. The ghost ship is just a legend of the swamp."

Even still, I did not plan on going out there at night. I didn't want to be the first fisherman captured by a pirate who doesn't exist.

Just then, my mom came out of the back bedroom. She was holding out some socks with a pair of pliers and had them out far away from her body.

"Whose socks are these?" she asked. "They smell like they've been worn for a week!"

"Umm, those are mine, Mrs. Pinner," said Bobber sheepishly. "I was in such a rush to get packed that I forgot

Flounder

Average length: 12 – 18 inches   Average weight: 2 – 4 pounds
Bait: shrimp, mullet, jigs or spoons fished near the bottom
Southern flounder have both eyes on the left side of their bodies
Also known as fluke, flattie, flatfish, doormat

to put any extra socks in my suitcase. I've been wearing those socks the whole trip. They were making my feet smell, so I took them off."

"Then it's time to stop and get you some new socks," said mom. "We're only a couple of hours away now."

"A couple of hours?" said Bobber as he motioned me towards the stairs that led up to one of the bubble canopies on the roof of the Zephyr. "Grab your goggles, Spinner, and let's go topside. I'm the famous pirate Stinky La-Feet from White Bear Lake, Minnesota, and I'm sailing this ship all the way to Louisiana!"

Stinky La-Feet
(a.k.a. Bobber)

Chapter 3

Action Galore
at the Tackle Store

The air brakes on the Zephyr let out a loud *WHOOSH!* as we came to a stop in the RV parking area of The Big Tackle Box just outside Lafitte. It sounded like the Zephyr was saying "Whew," like it was happy to take a rest.

Bobber and I worked our way down the stairs as The Chief, my mom and dad, and Uncle Pete stepped out into the parking lot. Uncle Pete walked around behind the Zephyr to check on *The Water Zephyr* and to make sure all the tires on both rigs were in good shape.

"This is bigger than a supermarket!" exclaimed Bobber.

The Chief told us that the store had all sorts of wildlife mounts, an aquarium, a restaurant, and even an indoor archery range. And they had HUGE fishing and boating departments.

"I'm heading for the sock department first," replied Bobber, pointing to his bare feet inside his Crocs. "I'm tired of being the famous pirate Stinky La-Feet."

"Bobber, you read my mind," said my mom. Everyone nodded in agreement while taking in and enjoying the fresh air outside the RV.

"Well, I'm heading for the camping department to see about that tent," announced The Chief.

"Spinner, you go with your dad and Uncle Pete to the fishing department while I take Bobber to the clothing department. We'll all meet at the aquarium in 45 minutes," said Mom as she and Bobber grabbed a shopping cart and headed inside.

When the sliding doors opened, we all entered the store together. I fell silent as I took in the size and scale of this mega outdoor gear store. I looked over at my friend. It seemed like Bobber's feet had stopped working. Then, his legs got all wobbly. Sweat began to bead on his forehead and his jaw fell open.

"Bobber, are you okay?" asked The Chief. "You look like you did when you first saw the Monster of White Bear Lake."

Monster of White Bear Lake

Huge muskie named Old Sam – read The Monster of White Bear Lake to learn how I caught him

We all stared at Bobber who had turned white and appeared frozen in his tracks. Now, Bobber is my best friend, and I know him better than anyone else. I could tell he was brewing up some classic Bobber enthusiasm.

So, I said to everyone, "Wait for it . . ."

"Wait for what?" asked Uncle Pete.

Then Bobber jumped into the air, pumping his fist. "I LOVE this place!" he shouted. "It's ginormous. It's super-duper stupendous. It's like the Super Bowl of Fishing Tackle!"

In front of me was a wall of fishing shirts, pants, hats and jackets, and to one side was aisle after aisle of fishing gear. Behind that were aisles filled with kayaks and behind that a boat showroom. And that was just one side of the store. On the other side was a hunting section, and next to that was a restaurant with an airplane hanging from the ceiling. In every direction there were animal mounts. I could also see a video shooting gallery next to one wall.

"Spinner, Spinner, this must be Heaven," said Bobber, jumping up and down until his shoes slipped off his stinky feet.

"No, boys. Heaven is where we're going fishing," said my dad with a smile.

We all went our separate ways as planned, and forty five minutes went by in a blur of outdoor awesomeness. My dad spent the entire time looking at fly rods while I spent the time looking at all the saltwater lures. Uncle Pete went over to the

RV section and came back with some electrical switches and blue LED light strips he planned to put on the steps of the Zephyr.

Just then, The Chief, my mom, and Bobber walked up pushing a shopping cart. Inside the cart were two new tents, a camp cot, and the biggest bag of beef jerky I've ever seen. Bobber held up three pairs of socks.

"These babies have odor-eating technology. I am no longer the famous Minnesota pirate Stinky La-Feet," said Bobber.

"Finally, I can breathe again," Uncle Pete gasped, and we all laughed at his joke.

I took Bobber over to the fishing section to show him all the gear. As we looked around, he jabbered on and on about all the cool features of the new tent. We must have gotten turned around, because when I looked back for everyone else, they were gone.

"Hey Bobber, I think we lost everyone," I said.

"Oh, no! They left us?" said Bobber as he looked up at the mount of a giant grizzly bear glaring ferociously down at us. "B-b-b-bear!"

Bobber struggled to get the next word out. "R-r-r-r-RUN!"

We both ran towards the front of the store, scrambling between aisles and away from all the mounted animals, and out into the open. As we got there, we spotted my mom in line at a cashier. She had a fishing rod in hand. Bobber and I ran over to her.

"Gee, Mrs. Pinner, I didn't know you planned on fishing, too," said Bobber.

"Oh sure, I used to go with my grandfather all the time," she said. "We would fill coolers with speckled trout. Then we'd come back home and clean them, and then we would eat peanut butter and jelly sandwiches together. He taught me everything I know."

"It's a family tradition," I said. "That's why my mom always packs peanut butter and jelly sandwiches in my lunch when we go fishing."

"And why all his fishing shirts have grape jelly stains on them," teased Bobber.

Chapter 4

Bayou Camp

As Uncle Pete steered the Zephyr through the streets of Lafitte, Bobber and I watched the buildings roll by from our view in the bubble canopy. From the top of the Zephyr, we could see a bunch of canals and an endless open marsh behind the buildings.

My mom talked on and on about her home state. I noticed her Louisiana accent was starting to work its way back into her voice. I love the sound of it. She pointed out Crawdaddy's, a small gas station with a sign that said "Live Bait" out front. She said they have the best po-boy sandwiches in town, and they open at 5 a.m., so we can gas up the boat and get bait at the same time. She told us that Crawdaddy's is also where all the fishing guides hang out.

"Sounds like the place we need to go for local fishing information," said Uncle Pete as he steered the Zephyr down a side street.

"For true!" said Mom.

The street led to a dirt road with large oak trees on one side and cypress trees on the other. Hanging from the branches were large clumps of Spanish moss that dangled toward the ground like a crusty old man's beard. It gave the trees a spooky look.

At the end of the road was an old, run-down cabin on a big lot of land with many great giant trees perfect for climbing on it. The back of the lot was on a canal with an old dock, and beyond that was the bayou as far as anyone could see. The Zephyr came to a stop at the back of the lot, right next to the well-used dock.

"We're here, boys," said Uncle Pete.

Bobber and I climbed down the ladder from the bubble canopy and were quickly out the door. Everyone else wasn't far behind. As we walked out onto the dock, there was a sign on one of the poles that read "Heaven."

"Heaven?" read Bobber, looking up at the sky. "Oh no! Did we die? I don't remember an accident," joked Bobber as he grabbed his chest and dramatically stumbled around.

"Oh, Bobber, you goof. Heaven was the name my grandfather gave this place," said my mom. "He always said this marsh was a little slice of Heaven on Earth."

Bobber and I knew exactly what she meant. Heaven to us was sitting on our docks together fishing and passing the time in White Bear Lake, Minnesota. That must be how this place made my great-grandfather feel.

My mom then explained that when she was a little girl, her grandfather, Charley Derbes, worked in New

Orleans and would take her here on weekends to get a break from the city. They would fish during the day and at night have big crawfish boils. I watched my mom on the dock remembering her past. I could feel how proud she felt to share her memories with us. I could even scrunch her down in my mind and picture her as a little kid standing on that dock.

She said the fishing in this area is so good that at times the shrimp are jumping out of the water and the gulls are diving, and there are so many speckled trout and redfish chasing them that you catch a fish on nearly every cast.

"Sure sounds like Heaven to me," said Bobber. "But I thought we were going to catch sea trout. What's a speckled trout?"

"Seatrout are the same thing as speckled trout," said my mom, and she explained that speckled trout was what the folks in Louisiana call them. "They have spots on

Speckled Trout

Average length: 14 - 18 inches   Average weight: 1 - 3 pounds
Bait: shrimp, mullet, croakers, and small fish like pogies
Silver and olive-green, with many small black dots
Actualy not a "trout" but a type of fish called a drum
Also called spotted sea trout, specks, yellowmouth

them and two big-fanged teeth in front. Redfish are fish that are red or copper in color, and both species live in the marsh, bayous, and bays. They're so abundant that some days you can catch a hundred of them."

"Well, I'm gonna be the Speckledest Trout Two-Fang Reddest Fish Champ of Heaven when this trip is over," said Bobber with authority.

"I believe you, Bobber," said my mom with a smile. "But first let's get the tents pitched and the boat in the water, and then maybe The Chief can take you boys out for an afternoon fishing trip."

That was the last thing we heard Mom say, because Bobber and I raced for the Zephyr, grabbed the tents, and started taking them out of their bags. My dad helped us spread them out. He read the instructions to us, and in no time we had two big tents set up near the dock under the shade of an old oak tree.

Shrimp

Average length: 4 – 5 inches

Crustaceans with claws and hard outer shells

Shrimp swim backwards, using their tails

Great for eating and also great for bait!

While we were setting up the tents, Uncle Pete and The Chief took the Zephyr to the boat ramp to launch *The Water Zephyr*. Bobber and I helped my dad build a campfire ring out of rocks while my mom set up a table in the shade of the tree.

"Lunch time, boys," she called as she set the plates and filled the cups with ice and lemonade. "Peanut butter and grape jelly sandwiches for everyone."

We all rushed over to the table, sat down, and started eating. Bobber must have been really hungry, because he ate his sandwich in four big bites.

"Thank you! That was the sweetest, grape-iest, peanut butter-iest sandwich in the world, Mrs. Pinner. You're the Butter Nutter Sandwich Champ," said Bobber with a sticky smile.

"Why, I'm glad you enjoyed it, Bobber," said my mom. "It's my family's own special recipe — peanut butter, jelly, and a little bit of lagniappe like powdered sugar tossed in for good measure." She turned her head towards the water and added, "Oh, look, here comes The Chief down the canal in the boat."

Cajun Dictionary

* for true - that's true

* lagniappe (pronounced "LAN-yap") - a little something extra; an unexpected surprise

Chapter 5

Big Help from a Little Shrimp

The Chief cut the engine, and *The Water Zephyr* slowly coasted up to the dock. He told us to grab our fishing rods.

"We'll use live shrimp for bait," said The Chief, "and put a Cajun Rattlin' Cork on to give it more casting distance and to draw the fish to the sound."

"The sound?" I said. "How does that work, Chief? I thought trout were sight feeders."

The Chief explained that Rattlin' Corks are made from wire with loops on both ends and a float in the middle with a bunch of glass or metal beads on either side. The wire has a lead weight on one end of the float which helps you cast the rig. More importantly, when you pull on the line, the beads bump into each other, and it makes a rattling sound similar to the sound shrimp make when they snap their bodies to jump.

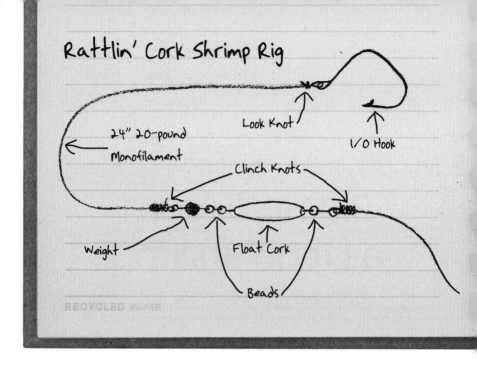

Rattlin' Cork Shrimp Rig

Look Knot

24" 20-pound Monofilament

1/0 Hook

Clinch Knots

Weight

Float Cork

Beads

"Oh, so the trout think they hear a shrimp nearby and swim over to the cork!" I said as I took out my FishingKids Notebook and drew a picture of the rig.

"That's right, Spinner. And when they get to the cork, they find the live shrimp we put below it on a baited hook. Just like your friend Coral showed you on our fishing trip to the Florida Keys, remember?" said The Chief with a wink.

"Well, rattle me up some jumping shrimp, I've got some trout to fool!" said Bobber. We grabbed our rods, tackle boxes, and FishingKids life jackets, and then headed for the boat.

As The Chief motored *The Water Zephyr* down the narrow canal, we passed a large shrimp boat named *Remy's Ride* that was tied to a dock. In the backyard was a dark-haired boy with camouflage shorts, a t-shirt, and white rubber boots, bouncing on a trampoline.

Shrimp
(a.k.a. Remy Terrebonne)

The end of the canal opened up into a huge bay, with a big island that had large sand hills on one side and large cypress trees filled with giant black birds on the other. Bobber called it "Vulture Island," and we both agreed that all those birds gave us the creeps.

Just then, the motor started running funny. It would go fast, then slow, and fast, and slow, until it wouldn't go fast anymore. The Chief turned off the engine and took the lid off the motor. He worked on the motor for ten minutes, but the engine still wouldn't speed up.

"Dat's not de problem," called the dark-haired boy from the trampoline, who had now walked to the end of the dock. "It's not de carburetors. It's de fuel water separator."

The Chief looked up curiously at the boy, who was now opening a duffel bag and pulling out tools. The Chief turned off the engine as wind pushed *The Water Zephyr* up to the dock where the boy was patiently waiting for us.

"Permission to board ya vessel, sir? They call me Shrimp, and I believe I can help y'all out," said the boy as he flashed a winning smile.

"Ah, sure," said The Chief, helping the boy aboard. "Are you qualified for such a job, Shrimp?"

"Yes, sir," Shrimp said proudly. "My daddy taught me everyting he knows. From de sounds of it, you gotta clogged fuel water separator. I can probably jus' clean it out for now, but y'all are gonna need a new one soon."

"Did you say your name was Shrimp?" asked Bobber.

"For true! But, ma given name's not Shrimp." He put out his hand to shake The Chief's. "Remy Terrebonne's my name, and eatin' a mess o' shrimp is my fame. That's how I came to be called Shrimp. Plus, I'm a whole head shorter den mos' kids my age." He began opening the engine hatch as he spoke.

Shrimp held up the filter and showed us the inside. It looked like it had toothpaste all over it. With a rag from his pocket, he cleaned out the white paste, screwed the filter back on, and asked The Chief to restart the motor. It turned over with the first crank. A smile spread across The Chief's weathered face.

The Chief asked Shrimp how he knew so much about boats. Shrimp gestured to the shrimp boat, *Remy's Ride*, which was tied up to the dock. "Ma daddy owns dat shrimpin' boat," he said. "I pay good attention to what he tells me, and he knows near everything 'bout boats. I like to help when I can, and when he's out shrimpin, I'm always fishin."

"We're going fishing right now," said The Chief. "Why don't you ask your father if you can join us?"

"Ooo-eee!" said Shrimp with delight. I looked at Bobber. We liked Shrimp immediately. Shrimp ran off towards his house and then came back with his fishing rod and jumped aboard. The Chief pointed *The Water Zephyr* out of the canal.

We entered Creole Bay, which was full of trout and redfish. As we neared the island to the southeast, we saw a whole flock of seagulls diving onto the water and grabbing the shrimp that were jumping out. The Chief cut the engine, and we drifted close to the action. He told us to hook the live shrimp.

No sooner had my bait hit the water than the cork went under. Bobber and Shrimp hooked up, too.

The next two hours went by in a blur, with The Chief baiting our hooks, taking off fish, and tossing them in the

Catch and Release

Hooking a fish and then letting it go. This is a way to conserve resources so that there will be fish to catch in the future.

boat, while we casted out and reeled them in. When one of us caught a small one, The Chief would take out the FishingKids Fish Ruler and measure it. If it was small, he'd throw it back.

We drifted across Creole Bay and close to the island Bobber called Vulture Island. Slowly, the seagulls started to disappear. When the birds were all gone, the fish stopped biting, too. Bobber and I looked at our feet, and there had to be 40 big speckled trout piled around them in the bottom of the boat.

"We're being attacked by trout!" joked Bobber, pretending to scoop up a fish and throw it overboard. "They're trying to sink the boat! Hey Chief, are we allowed to keep so many in one day?"

"You're allowed to keep 25 speckled trout per person," said The Chief. "Your mom wanted us to bring home a mess of trout so we could have a fish fry and invite the

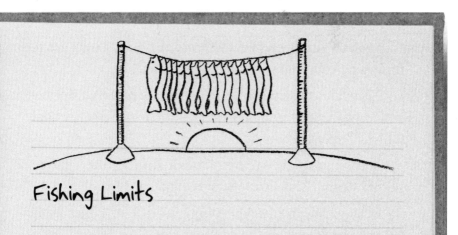

Fishing Limits

Maximum number and size of fish you're allowed to catch.

In Louisiana, the speckled trout limit is 25 fish per person per day, with a 12 inch minimum size limit, and only two of those fish can be more than 25 inches long.

neighbors. Remy, I hope you and your parents will come."

"If y'all are servin' shrimp with dose fish, I'll be dere," he said with a big grin.

The Chief was explaining the trout limits to Bobber and me when all the vultures on the island flew off at once. We watched the big black birds soaring in looping circles above the boat.

We were sitting in silence looking at the sky when Bobber yelled out, "Pirates! Pirates! Start the boat, Chief! Don't let the pirates get us!"

Bobber was pointing to the trees where the vultures had been. All The Chief, Shrimp, and I saw were trees.

"Calm down, Bobber," said The Chief. "I don't see anything."

"It's a pirate! I saw him! He had long hair, a scraggly beard, and earrings. He was covered with tattoos and had a mean scowl on his dirty face. He disappeared in the trees!"

"You've got pirates on the brain, Bobber. There are no pirates here anymore," noted The Chief.

"Then it's the ghost of Jean Lafitte," whispered Bobber, wide-eyed. "I saw him. Let's get out of here. Start the boat, Chief . . . please!"

"For true, some say dey've seen Jean Lafitte's ghost," said Shrimp. "And dey've seen it right in dis spot."

"Okay, Bobber, we're going," said The Chief as he turned the key, and the outboard on *The Water Zephyr* came to life. "We need to get back to camp before dark anyway."

Chapter 6

Jumbo Shrimp

"You look like you've seen a ghost, Bobber," said my mom as we unloaded *The Water Zephyr*.

"The Shrimp Boy fixed the boat and sea trout almost drowned us, and then vultures flew off with the disappearing pirate," said Bobber so fast and excitedly that you could barely understand him. "Pirates, Mrs. Pinner! There was a pirate on Vulture Island."

"Vulture Island? Pirates?" she replied. "Slow down, Bobber. I've never heard of Vulture Island."

"It's the island with all the trees on one side and sand hills on the other. Out in the bay," said Bobber.

"Oh, that's where the Lafittes live. You may have seen a descendant of a pirate, but Jean Lafitte has been dead for a long time. My grandfather liked to fish just west of that island," she said.

"That's where we fished today, Mom. We caught enough trout to feed an army," I said.

"Oh, ca c'est bon! We're gonna have a fais-do-do tonight!" she said as she clapped her hands.

Gee Mrs. Pinner, you sound just like a Cajun," said Bobber with astonishment. "What's a face dodo?"

"The more time I spend here, the more my accent comes back," said Mom. "A 'fais-do-do' is a Cajun dance party, usually late at night. I've invited all the neighbors, so there should be more children around. We'll stay up dancing and listening to Zydeco, and we'll eat fried trout and shrimp etouffee and oysters all night."

The Chief, Uncle Pete, and my dad took turns cleaning the trout while Bobber and I helped my mom set up the tables and chairs for our fais-do-do. It wasn't long before people started showing up.

The Chief and Uncle Pete had set up a big camp stove on one of the tables. One burner had a big pot of boiling

Cajun Dictionary

* Ca c'est bon. (pronounced "SA SAY BAWN") - That is good
* Ca viens? (pronounced "SA vee-AN") - It means, "Hello, how are you doing?"
* etouffee (pronounced "ay-too-FAY") - a creamy rice dish, usually with shrimp or crawfish
* y'all - you all, or you guys

oil and the other had a pot of boiling water. The Chief was frying fish while Uncle Pete was boiling shrimp.

"Shrimp are a staple of every Cajun party," said Uncle Pete as he popped a crustacean into his mouth. "This is shrimp country, and some of the biggest and best-tasting shrimp in the world come from these waters."

After I put the bowl of shrimp on the table, my mom asked Bobber and me to fill some glasses with iced tea and lemonade. We then helped The Chief put the fried fish on the table. Shrimp showed up wearing blue jean overalls, a blue T-shirt, and the same white rubber boots.

"Evenin', y'all," he said, holding out his hand. "Ca viens?"

"Huh?" said Bobber.

"What did you say?" I followed.

"Ca viens?" he said again. "It means, 'hello, how are ya doin'?"

"All these Cajun words are a lot different from what we would say in White Bear Lake, Minnesota," noted Bobber.

Shrimp laughed and told us we were the ones who sounded funny. "Can't barely understand y'all." I hadn't thought about the fact that we probably sounded strange to him.

Shrimp told us about the tradition of fais-do-do. I liked the way it brought all of the neighbors together, and how everyone seemed to be like one big family. Bobber said that he liked the music. "It's kind of like fast-playing music with an auctioneer for a singer," said Bobber.

"Zydeco, Cajun music. Goes wit de party. Now, let's get us some o' dose shrimp!" said Shrimp, as he piled a huge mound of shrimp on his plate. "I may not be big, but I eat a jumbo portion o' shrimp."

Shrimp wasn't kidding. He ate plate after plate of them. He ate so many that Bobber said he had two hollow legs, which made him laugh and say he needed to fill out his white boots.

We ate boiled shrimp and crawfish, fried fish, fried turkey, and all kinds of rice dishes. It all tasted different, and new, and . . . incredible. Even Bobber thought it was all good, especially the fried turkey, which he built into a giant mound on his plate. Bobber and I were trying everything we could get our hands on, that is, until the Hot Sauce Incident.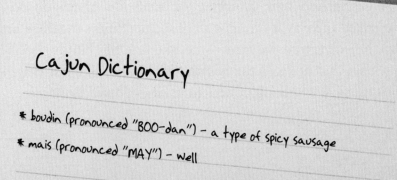

Cajun Dictionary

* boudin (pronounced "BOO-dan") - a type of spicy sausage
* mais (pronounced "MAY") - well

Chapter 7

Spicy Hot Bobber

Shrimp, Bobber, and I were eating more shrimp when my mom brought over a plate of sausages and put it on the table.

"Try this boudin, boys," she said. "It's some of the best in town."

"Oh boy, bratwurst!" said Bobber, stabbing one of the sausages with his fork and putting it on his plate. "I love brats."

"This is boudin. It's Cajun sausage," said my mom, as she took another plate over to the main table.

"Boo-dan?" said Bobber, as he poked at the giant sausage link with his fork. "I thought it looked too big to be a brat."

"Boudin is great, for true," said Shrimp. "One-third rice, one-third spice, and one-third pork, though I like shrimp boudin best, mais of course."

Bobber shrugged his shoulders and said, "Sausage is sausage in my book," and he grabbed a bottle of red liquid off the table and started shaking it on the boudin. "I like mine with lots of catsup on it."

"Dat's not catsup. Dat's Louisiana Hot Sauce," said Shrimp. "Only takes one drop ta spice up ya food. Boy, you may not wanna eat dat."

But it was too late. Bobber had cut a big piece of boudin and forked it into his mouth. Almost immediately, his face turned red, and tears came to his eyes. I could swear I saw smoke come out of his ears.

"Hot-fire-catsup-burning-sausage tongue!" yelled Bobber, and he ran through the party waving his arms over his head. "Call an ambulance! I have the catsup fire face!"

Everyone stopped dancing and watched as Bobber ran over to the faucet, turned it on, and started drinking from the hose.

"Hot, hot, hot," he gasped between gulps of water. "Not boo-dan, boo-danger. Do I still have a tongue?"

Everyone laughed and started dancing again, while Shrimp, Bobber, and I moved over to the camp and sat around the fire. Uncle Pete was working on installing the blue LED lights on the steps of the Zephyr. Shrimp saw him and wandered over. A few minutes later, Shrimp and Uncle Pete were working together and had the lights installed in no time.

In a little while, people started leaving the party, and Uncle Pete and my dad came over and sat by the fire with us. Shrimp said it was getting late, and he had to go home because his dad was going out in his boat shrimping the next day.

Shrimp explained that many families in Louisiana live off the bounty of the land and Gulf, eating some of what they catch and selling the rest. The marsh was so rich with shrimp, fish, and other wildlife that the next meal was always just around the next canal.

We sat in chairs around the fire ring, and Uncle Pete told us about his flying missions while my dad talked about building bridges. Then Uncle Pete said he was turning in. As he went into his tent, my dad went over to the Zephyr to say good night to my mom and The Chief.

Bobber and I were sitting by the fire and looking out over the marsh when a small boat appeared silently from the darkness. The boat looked like a wide canoe with a man standing in the middle and holding a long wooden pole. He used the pole to push the boat along silently.

As it passed our camp, the light from the fire allowed us to see the man on board. He had long, stringy hair, a dark face with lots of tattoos on his arms, and a red bandana around his neck. And where he held the wooden pole, instead of a hand, he had a long, curved, pointed, shiny, metal hook. He looked . . . exactly . . . like a . . . pirate.

Bobber and I jumped up from our seats. "The pirates are attacking! The pirates are attacking! It's the ghost of

Jean Lafitte!" yelled Bobber as we ran towards the Zephyr.

"I saw him, Bobber. I saw the pirate, too," I gulped, and we banged on the door to the RV.

"What's the matter, boys?" said my dad as he opened the door. "See a ghost?"

"Yes, Mr. Pinner," replied Bobber, out of breath. "As a matter of fact, we did. It was the pirate ghost of Jean Lafitte. He was just over by the fire."

"You boys have had too much to eat," said my dad. "I don't see anyone."

"It's true, Dad. I saw it, too. He had a hook for a hand and was covered with tattoos. I saw it, Dad," I said and shivered.

"Hmm, a pirate with a hook for a hand," said my dad. "We'll have to look into this more tomorrow."

Chapter 8

Shop Talk

After seeing the pirate, I don't think I slept a wink all night. I was lying in my sleeping bag when I heard *The Water Zephyr's* engine start.

Thinking it might be the pirate trying to steal our boat, I got up quickly and peeked through the flaps of the tent. Standing on the dock in the dark was Uncle Pete. I dressed quickly and walked out to the dock.

"Good morning, Uncle Pete," I said as I rubbed my eyes. "Are you going fishing?"

"No, I'm just heading up the canal to Crawdaddy's," he replied. "I thought I'd pick up some live shrimp and see if I can get some reliable fishing information from the guides. Want to come along?"

"Sure," I said, looking back at the tent where Bobber and my dad were still sleeping.

"We'll be back before they wake up," he said. "Hop in, and let's get going. The sun will be up soon."

On the ride up the canal, I kept watching for the pirate ghost as I told Uncle Pete about his appearance near our camp. Uncle Pete said the boat sounded like a pirogue, a small one- or two-man boat common in the Louisiana marsh.

It was only about a half mile up the canal to Crawdaddy's. We pulled up to the big dock alongside four or five fishing boats, tied off, and walked inside. As we entered the shop from the rear, I could hear all the men inside having a loud discussion.

One wall of Crawdaddy's was covered with fishing tackle, mostly soft plastic shrimp and jigs along with some hooks and Cajun Rattlin' Corks. Another wall had a meat counter and sandwiches, and a tray of boudin. There were duck decoys and frog gigs and crab nets and an entire row of white rubber boots. The discussion got louder as we walked over to the shrimp tank.

"Juste Terrebonne goin' out again t-day," said one man. "You'd tink he'd take Bayou Boudreaux wit him. You know, jes for hep'n out."

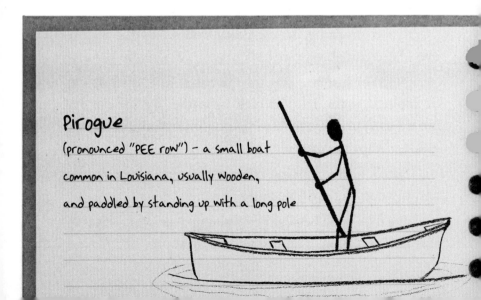

Pirogue
(pronounced "PEE row") – a small boat common in Louisiana, usually wooden, and paddled by standing up with a long pole

"Bayou Boudreaux don' want to go shrimpin, or fishin for dat matter. Since de accident, he don' want to do nothin' but feel sorry for himself," said another.

"In his day, Bayou Boudreaux could catch a limit of specks in a hurricane," said the man behind the counter. "It's a shame what happened to him. Dere never was a better fisherman in dis marsh."

"Yeah, you right," said the man who made the first comment. "Juste would do anyting to pay him back, but Boudreaux says he don' want any charity, not even from his best friends." The men all shook their heads.

"Bayou Boudreaux knows every inch of dis marsh, but he can't catch a single fish," said the man behind the counter. "Guess I'd give up de life, too."

When there was a break in their conversation, Uncle Pete stepped up and asked how the fish were biting and for six dozen live shrimp. The man behind the counter told us that the five-gallon bucket we were using was a death trap for our shrimp, and we should put them in a Flow Troll Bucket® so they would stay alive all day. While

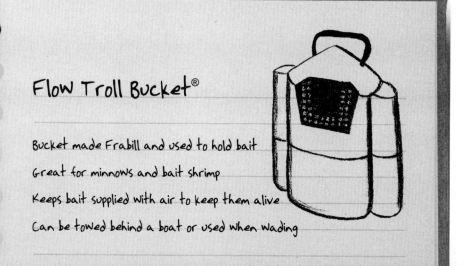

Flow Troll Bucket®

Bucket made Frabill and used to hold bait
Great for minnows and bait shrimp
Keeps bait supplied with air to keep them alive
Can be towed behind a boat or used when wading

he filled our new bucket, the others gave Uncle Pete some fishing advice.

We grabbed our Flow Troll Bucket® and jumped in the boat. By the time we motored down the canal and back to camp, my dad had a fire going. Bobber was heading for the dock with his fishing rod. He was there to meet us when we arrived.

"Your dad and The Chief are going out fishing with your Uncle Pete while we fish from the dock," said Bobber. "Shrimp said there are flounder, speckled trout, and redfish in this canal. He's going to come over later and show us his secret fish-catching rig."

Chapter 9

The Treasure of Creole Bay

Shrimp showed up at our camp just as my dad, The Chief, and Uncle Pete were leaving. Bobber and I grabbed our rods and headed over to the dock to fish. That's when Shrimp pulled out his secret lure to show us.

"Dat's de Coccahoe Minnow," said Shrimp as he held up a small black plastic lure with a chartreuse colored boot-type tail. "De Cocchahoe is de best lure in de bayou, for true."

"The cock-a-doodle minnow?" inquired Bobber. "Looks like a swimbait to me."

"It does look like a swimbait, only it's a little fatter," I said to Shrimp as I took out my FishingKids Notebook and drew a picture of the lure. "We have some lures in our tackle box that we use on White Bear Lake for smallmouth bass that look sort of the same."

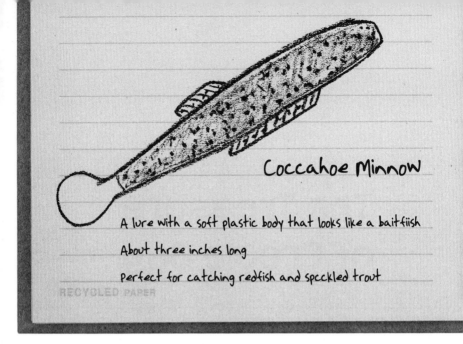

Coccahoe Minnow

A lure with a soft plastic body that looks like a baitfiish

About three inches long

Perfect for catching redfish and speckled trout

"Coccahoe," he replied with force. "Mud minnow, killifish. Dey all over de marsh. Dis Coccahoe has a quarter-ounce jighead. Y'all wanna use red, cause it looks like de minnow is injured," said Shrimp as he held up the red, black, and chartreuse combination.

"You use the coccadoodle," said Bobber as he bent over and pulled off one of his Crocs and pointed to the lure imbedded in it. "I'll use my lucky Shoe Bait!"

When we were fishing in Minnesota last summer, Bobber got a lure stuck in his Croc by accident, and he decided it was a good luck charm. He now keeps a lure in his shoe at all times, and uses it to fish with when he needs a secret weapon.

We fished off the dock for about an hour and didn't catch a thing. Shrimp didn't get a bite on his Coccahoe Minnow,

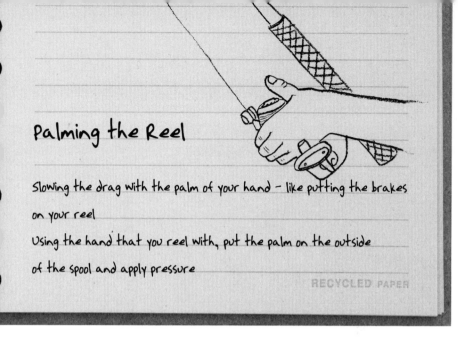

Palming the Reel

Slowing the drag with the palm of your hand – like putting the brakes on your reel

Using the hand that you reel with, put the palm on the outside of the spool and apply pressure

RECYCLED PAPER

and Bobber's Shoe Bait went fishless. After a while, Shrimp suggested we walk to the point just past his house and fish in Creole Bay.

"De tide's not moving enough in de canal," he said. "We need us some movin' water if we gonna catch some fish."

We asked my mom, and she said it was fine to walk to the point, but to be back for lunch. It took us ten minutes of fast walking to get there.

The point was a small section of beach where the canal opened into the bay. We could see the water moving and birds diving. Along the shoreline, minnows were jumping out of the water as fish chased them against the beach. We knew right away we were going to catch fish.

On his first cast, Shrimp hooked something big that was taking out line from his reel. He put his fingers on the reel spool to add some extra drag and slow the fish down. When the fish stopped, he started pumping in line.

"That was cool, Shrimp. I've never seen that before," I said, pointing to his hand on the spool of the reel.

"Dat's called palmin' de reel," he replied. "You do it to add a lil' extra drag, but you have to take your fingers off the reel if de fish makes a hard run, or you'll break de line."

It took a while, but with Bobber and I coaching him and Shrimp palming the reel, he finally brought the fish close to shore where its copper-colored back stuck out of the water.

"Grab a stick, Spinner! It's an armored car fish," said Bobber as he stepped back from shore.

"Dat's redfish," said Shrimp as he casually led the fish to the beach. "He's covered wit big scales dat look like body armor. Looks 'bout 15 pounds, so tis a good one for true, but too big to keep."

"Too big!" said Bobber." "There's enough fish there to have another face doe-doe tonight."

"You can keep five redfish each day, but dey have to be 'tween 16 and 26 inches. Though you can keep one big one if you want," said Shrimp as he pulled his lure from the fish's mouth and let it swim off. "We like de smaller ones. Dese big ones are too fishy-tastin for me and ma daddy."

"I want to catch a giant armored car!" said Bobber, making a cast with his Shoe Bait.

For the next 30 minutes, Shrimp caught redfish, speckled trout, and flounder on just about every cast, while I caught two trout on live shrimp and Bobber never got a bite on his Shoe Bait. We were beginning to get frustrated and were about to admit that Shrimp's lure was the best bait for the marsh, when Bobber's rod doubled over.

"Giant! Giant! I've got a truck-sized armored car redfish!" he said, as he pulled back on the rod and slowly gained line.

Shrimp and I stopped fishing and watched as Bobber pulled hard on the fish.

"I told you guys, it's the Shoe Bait," he said as he fought the weight on the other end of the line. "It may not catch a lot of fish, but it sure catches the biggest."

Shrimp and I had to agree that Bobber had certainly hooked into a something that weighed a lot. As he slowly worked it to shore, we noticed it wasn't fighting very hard. He'd pull back and move the fish, but the fish never pulled out line. That's when we saw the top of the chest.

"What kind of brown flat-headed fish is that?" said Bobber as he continued to pull back on his fishing rod.

"That's not a fish. It's some kind of chest," I said, and then spun around towards Bobber with excitement. "Maybe it's a pirate's treasure!"

We all stood still with our jaws open. Bobber had just reeled in a chest about two feet wide and a foot tall with a lock on the side. Just like the kind the pirates used.

"It's the treasure of Jean Lafitte! My Shoe Bait must have smelled it! We're gonna be rich!" shrieked Bobber. We waded into the water and grabbed the treasure chest.

Chapter 10

Parade Gazillionaires

It took all the strength Shrimp, Bobber, and I could muster to carry the treasure chest out of the water. When we got to shore, we placed the chest on the beach. Bobber tried to open it, but the chest was locked.

"Aw, cheese and crackers!" said Bobber. "It won't open."

"Lemme try," said Shrimp. He pulled a long, curved piece of steel out of his back pocket.

"What's that?" I asked, pointing to the blunt tool.

"Dat's an oyster shuckin' knife. We

use it to open de oyster shells. It might be strong enough to pry de chest open," replied Shrimp as he wedged the tool between the top and bottom of the chest.

With a little prying, and with Bobber and me pulling on the lid, we finally made a big enough gap for Shrimp to push the tool into the opening. Shrimp took a deep breath, straightened his arms, and then pushed down quickly.

"Pop!" went the trunk lid as it opened.

"You did it!" I shouted.

"It's all 'bout technique," Shrimp said confidently as he lifted the lid to the chest. We held our breaths, peered inside, and we all saw that it was filled to the top with gold coins!

"I'm a gazillionaire!" yelled Bobber. "I found the treasure of Jean Lafitte! I'm going to buy a hundred bajillion Shoe Baits and catch all the treasure chests in Louisiana!"

Bobber started hopping up and down and waving his arms as he continued to holler.

"Call the banks. Call the newspapers. Call the police! I'm going to need a wheelbarrow for all this money!" he shouted.

While Bobber ran around excitedly looking for something to carry the gold coins, Shrimp leaned in and picked up one of the coins. Then he put it to his mouth and squeezed it between his teeth.

"Bobber, Bobber, dose are Mardi Gras doubloons," he said, shaking his head.

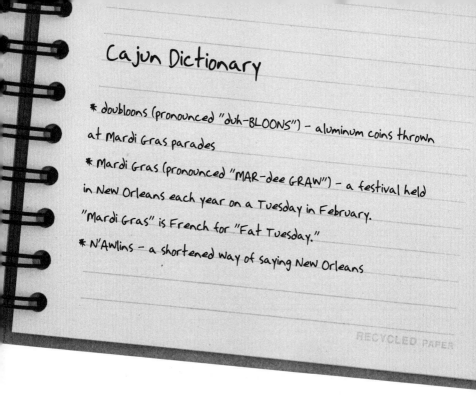

Cajun Dictionary

* doubloons (pronounced "duh-BLOONS") — aluminum coins thrown at Mardi Gras parades
* Mardi Gras (pronounced "MAR-dee GRAW") — a festival held in New Orleans each year on a Tuesday in February. "Mardi Gras" is French for "Fat Tuesday."
* N'Awlins — a shortened way of saying New Orleans

"Marty Graw's Doubloons! Did you hear that Spinner? I found Marty Graw's Doubloons," said Bobber.

"No, no, Mardi Gras doubloons," he said, shaking his full head of dark hair. "Dey are no treasure. Dey are aluminum coins from de Mardi Gras parades in N'Awlins. Dey is worthless."

"Worthless?" said Bobber and he stopped in his tracks. "Even you said they're gold doubloons. They have to be worth something."

Shrimp explained that the doubloons were just trinkets from the Mardi Gras parades in New Orleans. Mardi Gras is a big carnival with costumes and parades. The people on the floats throw beads and gold coins called doubloons. Some kid must have filled a chest with them and dropped it in the water. Maybe even as a joke. It sort of sounded to me like the type of prank Bobber would pull.

"You mean I'm not going to be rich and buy a tractor trailer full of Shoe Baits?" asked Bobber.

"No Shoe Baits," replied Shrimp. "Jus' some fake coins dat look like real pirate treasure."

Bobber looked crushed. "Wow, for a minute there, I thought we found the treasure that the ghost pirate was after," said Bobber. "That's why he came by our camp."

"Ghost pirate?" inquired Shrimp. "Dere is no ghost pirate 'round he'ah."

We told Shrimp about the pirate we had seen on two different occasions. Each time we spotted him, he had disappeared without a sound.

"He's got one good arm and one with a big hook on it," explained Bobber.

When he mentioned the arm with the hook, Shrimp perked up.

"Dat sounds like Boudreaux Lafitte," he said. "His great, great, great granddaddy was de pirate Jean Lafitte — de meanest, scariest pirate in all of Louisiana."

Chapter 11

Bayou Boys

My dad, Uncle Pete, and The Chief came in from their morning of fishing just as we got back to Heaven. Bobber and I emptied the doubloons from our pockets as my mom walked up to say that lunch was ready.

As we walked over to the tables, we told everyone about the pirate's chest and the big redfish that Shrimp had caught. My dad said the fishing in Creole Bay was not very good where they went. They only caught two small trout.

"Maybe Spinner, Bobber, Shrimp, and I will go back out after lunch and see if we can catch some fish for dinner," said The Chief.

"I don't know, Chief," said my dad. "It's starting to cloud up. It'll probably rain this afternoon."

"The overcast conditions will cool things off and make the fishing better," replied The Chief as he shrugged off

the approaching weather. "We'll have our life jackets on at all times, so there's really not much to worry about."

"Why don't you go right now?" said my mom. "I'll pack you some sandwiches while you load the gear. But you have to promise to head back in if it looks like it's going to storm."

Bobber, Shrimp, and I grabbed our fishing rods and headed for the dock, while The Chief got the FishingKids life jackets. My mom brought us a bag of sandwiches that The Chief put in the cooler. Then he started the engine, and we motored out of the canal.

The Chief headed toward the island in Creole Bay. When he cut the engine, we could see the sand hills nearby.

"This is right near where we caught them yesterday, Chief," I said as I got my rod ready to cast, "although we're closer to that island than we were with Uncle Pete."

"That's the pirate island of Boudreaux Lafitte, right Shrimp?" said Bobber.

"I wouldn't worry much about pirates, boys," noted The Chief. "I'd be more concerned with why your Cajun Rattlin' corks are no longer on the surface."

With that, we all set our hooks at the same time. Bobber yanked back so hard, he knocked the hat off his head with his fishing rod.

Bobber missed the fish that ate his bait, but my fishing rod bent nearly double, and Shrimp reeled a small speckled trout to the boat and released it. My fish took out line, and I used the palm of my hand to add drag to the reel, just like Shrimp had showed me. In a little while, and with some coaching from Shrimp, I had the fish to the boat.

"Wow, look at the size of that flounder," said The Chief in amazement.

Bobber and I were both leaning over the side trying to get a better look at the fish when Shrimp leaned over with the net, scooped it up, and hauled it into the boat.

"Holy alien bug-eyed flatfish! It's got both eyes on the same side of its head," hollered Bobber.

"Yes, the Southern flounder is a left-facing flounder that has both eyes on the same side of its body," noted The Chief. "That's so it can lay flat on the bottom and still see its food swimming above it."

Bobber re-baited with a shrimp, cast out, and immediately caught a speckled trout.

"Game on," he said. But, for the next 45 minutes, we never got another bite. Even Shrimp's special Coccahoe Minnow lure and Bobber's lucky Shoe Bait let us down.

We were so caught up in fishing that we hadn't noticed that the clouds had started to build and the sky had gotten darker. We weren't paying much attention to the approaching storm until the wind picked up against our backs, making us all turn around. Behind us was a giant wall of low clouds and dark, pelting rain.

"Dose storm clouds," said Shrimp. "It's a-comin in hot!"

"We need to get out of here in a hurry, boys," The Chief said. I reeled in my fishing rod and stowed it.

The wind started blowing harder, and the open bay was getting rough as waves started to crash into *The Water Zephyr*. The Chief tried to start the engine while Bobber, Shrimp, and I made sure everything was lashed down tight. The engine started, but the wind was blowing from the side, and that allowed water to come in the boat any time we pointed it back towards Heaven.

"It's too rough," said The Chief over the loud, gusting wind. "I'm going to make a run for that island. We can get out of the wind behind it, and then we'll head for home after the storm blows through."

"But Chief, that's Vulture Island," said Bobber as he shook his head. "That's where the pirate lives."

"Not Vulture Island, dat's Boudreaux Lafitte's Island," said Shrimp as he held on to the side of the boat to keep from rocking overboard.

"It's the only safe place right now, boys," replied The Chief. "Vultures, pirates, or not, we're heading there."

Chapter 12

Pirate's Quarters

The ride to the island was scary, with waves breaking around us and the rain right on our tails. As we got close to the island, the bay got rougher and waves were crashing on the shore. We all started to worry.

We motored around the island, close to the tall trees that held all those vultures the day before, and the same place where we first spotted the pirate. The wind blew through the trees, and the Spanish moss started falling from the limbs. It looked like spider webs were falling on us from the sky as we headed for the back side of the island.

Once we passed the sand hills, the wind let up, but the rain was still approaching. The Chief spotted a small cabin on the shore with a dock. He pulled *The Water Zephyr* up to it as the rain started coming down.

77

"Grab the cooler, and run for that fishing shack. I'll tie the boat off," said The Chief over the sound of the wind and rain.

We rushed down the dock and were just to the porch of the cabin, when the door flew open. The pirate stepped out.

"What 'er you boys doin' on ma island?" he roared, stopping the three of us in our tracks.

It wasn't the sight of the stringy hair, hoop earring, or bandana across the pirate's head that made Bobber turn back towards the dock. It was the big, hook-like clamp on his arm where a hand would normally be. It was curved with a black metallic sheen, and the points looked freshly sharpened. Bobber was about to run, when I grabbed his shirt.

"Excuse me, sir," I said with conviction. "We were caught in the storm and couldn't make it back in. So we headed here to get out of the wind and rain. My grandfather is securing the boat on the dock."

The pirate looked Bobber and me up and down. Shrimp was standing behind Bobber, so the pirate couldn't see him. He then lifted his head towards the dock where The Chief was just stepping out of the boat. He leaned forward with his sharp, pointed, hooked hand and slowly slid it under a bucket handle.

"Well den, y'all come on in," he said as he lifted the handle of the bucket and motioned for us to follow him.

I thought Bobber had stepped in a bucket of cement, because I couldn't move him. I was pulling on his shirt, trying to move forward, but he wasn't moving. Shrimp

wasn't saying anything either, just staring at the pirate. Just then, The Chief walked up.

"You boys better get in out of the rain," he said, nodding at the man in the doorway and extending his hand. "I'm Chester Pinner. The boys call me The Chief."

The man in the doorway put down the bucket and extended his hook-like hand. "Boudreaux Lafitte," he said as he spotted Shrimp for the first time. "Folks call me Bayou Boudreaux."

The Chief took the pirate's hook in his hand and shook it. Bobber's jaw just about dropped to the floor.

"You're the famous fishing guide Bayou Boudreaux?" asked The Chief.

"Mais, I used to be," he said as he turned and walked inside with us following him. "Dat was before de accident. Now, I can't hold a fishin rod no more."

"Gee, we thought you were a pirate. That you were going to capture us and cut us into little pieces to use us as crab bait, so we couldn't find your buried treasure," said Bobber.

"Funny you say dat. Dese sand hills are where ma great-great-granddaddy Jean Lafitte used to bury some o' his gold," said Bayou Boudreaux. "And I guess I might look a lot like a pirate wit dis long hair an' bandana. I have a hard time brushin ma hair wit only one hand."

We all smiled at his joke as the rain started coming down so hard it sounded like drums beating on his metal roof. Bayou Boudreaux looked out the window of his fishing shack. Then he stared at Shrimp for a long time before he decided to speak.

"Dat's a bad un," he said. "It bes y'all wait it out he'ah. Wan some mud bugs?"

"Mud bugs?" said Bobber. "You mean for bait?

"No, mud bugs . . . crawfish. I got a whole bucket o' dem dis morn'n," he said as he leaned the bucket forward and let us look in. Inside, it was piled high with crawfish.

"Only if you'll have one of my mom's sandwiches," I said. "She makes the best peanut butter and grape jelly sandwiches in the world."

Bayou Boudreaux cooked up a pot full of crawfish, covered the table with newspaper, and poured them out on the table. He then showed us how to pinch the heads off them and eat the tails. For Bobber and me, eating crawfish was a new thrill.

I opened the cooler and pulled out all the sandwiches my mom had made. I cut them into fours, and I put them all on a plate. We then ate crawfish and peanut butter and grape jelly sandwiches.

"Ya know, Spinner, dese sandwiches are not bad," he said with respect. "Dey remind me o' Charley Derbes over down Heaven. He made da sweet sandwiches like dis, too. And he never went fishin without 'em."

"Charley Derbes?" I said. "That's my mom's grandfather."

With that, Bayou Boudreaux burst into a big smile.

"I thought you looked kinda like him," he said.

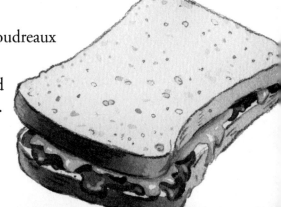

"Mais, any family 'a Charley Derbes is a good friend o' mine."

"Dat boy wit de dark hair — the peeshwank. He's Cajun for true. He got de face of a Terrebonne," said Bayou Boudreaux.

"I'm Remy Terrebonne, sir," said Shrimp. "Juste's son. You saved my daddy's life."

Cajun Dictionary

* ax – ask

* cher (pronounced "SHARE") – my dear

* peeshwank – a small person (like a "pipsqueak")

A Pirate in Need

From that point on, Bayou Boudreaux told us fishing stories, cooked crawfish, and ate peanut butter and jelly sandwiches while we all sat at the table and listened. He paused and then looked out in the distance. "But dat was before I had de accident."

"Is that when you lost your hand?" asked Bobber, pointing to the sharp metal hook at the end of Bayou Boudreaux's arm.

"Now Bobber, let's respect Mr. Lafitte's privacy," said The Chief.

"No, no, dat's no problem," said Bayou Boudreaux. "It's a story for true."

He then told us the story of the hurricane of August 2005, and how Juste Terrebonne's shrimp boat blew up on the island as the storm approached. Bayou Boudreaux swam out to the boat to help untangle Juste from the shrimp nets that fell on him when the boom broke.

Bayou Boudreaux had just gotten Juste out of the net, when a big wave swept the entire net overboard. The line tangled around his hand, and the weight of the net tore the rope into his wrist and fingers. It did so much damage to his hand that it almost cut it completely off. It finally pulled free, but then Juste had to help Bayou Boudreaux get back to the island.

They spent five days on the island before the storm let up and the water receded enough for a rescue boat to reach them. During that time, Bayou Boudreaux's hand got infected and couldn't be saved.

"But your daddy gotta live, so I am happy for dat," he said to Shrimp. "Mais, I can't do charters no more. I can't hold a fishing rod wit dis hook."

"That's too bad," I said. "I wish there was something we could do to help."

The Chief shook his head. I could tell he was thinking the same thing as the sun popped through the clouds. We stepped outside and realized that the wind had let up. The skies were starting to clear.

"Dat's how de storms are on de bayou," said Bayou Boudreaux as he pointed to the sky. "Dey come in quick, and dey leave jus as quick."

We all thanked Bayou Boudreaux for letting us stay in his shack out of the storm, and for all the good food. Then we climbed into *The Water Zephyr*. The Chief started the engine, and we headed for home on calmer waters.

Back at camp, we showed my mom and dad and Uncle Pete the giant flounder, and we told them the story of

Bayou Boudreaux. Everyone was surprised to hear that the Pirate of Creole Bay was an old fishing guide who had an accident and now couldn't fish anymore. Mom loved that he knew her grandfather, and that he liked her peanut butter and jelly sandwiches.

After dinner, we were all sitting around the camp rigging fishing rods for the next day when Shrimp walked up. He was holding a big spring that was attached to a belt with duct tape.

"What'cha got there, Shrimp?" I asked.

"It's a tool so Bayou Boudreaux can go fishin again. It attaches to his arm below de hook so he can hold a fishin rod," said Shrimp.

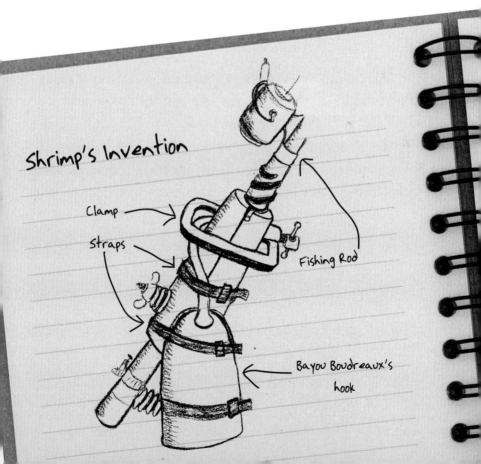

Shrimp's Invention

Clamp

Straps

Fishing Rod

Bayou Boudreaux's hook

Shrimp then explained to us how the contraption would work. Bayou Boudreaux would be able to strap on the device just below his wrist, and put the end of the fishing rod in it. The rod above the reel would be held inside the hook he already has. Then, he would be able to cast with that arm and reel with his good hand.

Shrimp then handed the tool to my dad, and he and The Chief looked it over and started talking about it in low whispers. They told Shrimp that the design he came up with might just work, but that they were going to work on it and see if they could improve it so it wouldn't break under the pressure of a big fish.

"That's a pretty impressive prosthesis you designed, Shrimp," said my dad.

"Whoa, that's cool!" added Bobber. "Do you really think it will work?

"All we can do is try, boys," said my dad, "but it looks like it might do the job. Now let's run into town and see if we can find all the parts we need."

We all raced to the Zephyr, excited to be a part of trying to help Bayou Boudreaux once again become the best fishing guide in Lafitte.